A ROOKIE READER®

ELLIOT
DRIVES AWAY

By Matt Curtis

Illustrations by Jenny Williams

SCHOLASTIC INC.

New York Toronto London Auckland Sydney
Mexico City New Delhi Hong Kong Buenos Aires

For Carrol R. Curtis

ISBN 0-516-24191-5

Copyright © 1996 by Children's Press®, Inc. All rights reserved.
Published by Scholastic Inc., 557 Broadway, New York, NY 10012.
SCHOLASTIC and associated logos are trademarks
and/or registered trademarks of Scholastic Inc.

12 11 10 9 8 7 6 5 4 3 2 1   3 4 5 6 7 8/0

Printed in the U.S.A.   61

First Scholastic printing, May 2003

Elliot had had enough!
Enough of his vegetables, enough
cleaning his room, and enough
of his bully big brother.

So he slipped behind the
wheel of his toy car

and drove away.

Pill bugs, worms, centipedes,
twigs the size of logs —

the dangers seemed as large as the sky.

An earwig

he fought with a stick.

A rat he bribed

with some cheese.

A blue jay he scared
with a terrible scream.

"I'm getting away!"
he cried,

and sped up his car.

Then he
crashed

into the root
of a tree.

But that didn't stop Elliot,
who marched on

through a jungle of grass.

He scaled sprinkler tops
with a harness and rope.

He scouted
mole holes with
a helmet and light.

He floated
rapids on an
old piece of bark.

In the evening,
he set up camp under
a fern, keeping watch
against aphids and slugs.

But
a daddy longlegs,

28

with its long, kinked legs
working like cranes,
carried Elliot home—

to dinner.

Word List (108 Words)

a	cranes	holes	piece	stop
against	crashed	home	pill	terrible
an	cried	I'm	rapids	that
and	daddy	in	rat	the
aphids	dangers	into	room	then
as	didn't	its	root	through
away	dinner	jay	rope	to
bark	drove	jungle	scaled	tops
behind	earwig	keeping	scared	toy
big	Elliot	kinked	scouted	tree
blue	enough	large	scream	twigs
bribed	evening	legs	seemed	under
brother	fern	light	set	up
bugs	floated	like	size	vegetables
bully	fought	logs	sky	watch
but	getting	long	slipped	wheel
camp	grass	longlegs	slugs	who
car	had	marched	so	with
carried	harness	mole	some	worms
centipedes	he	of	sped	working
cheese	helmet	old	sprinkler	
cleaning	his	on	stick	

About the Author ···

Matt Curtis lives with his wife in Salt Lake City, Utah, where he eagerly anticipates the day when he can read a story of his own— to a child of his own!

About the Illustrator ···

Jenny Williams was born and educated in London, where she studied at the Wimbledon School of Art and at London University. Starting as a magazine and advertising illustrator, she soon discovered that illustrating children's books was what she loved doing best. She has illustrated countless books ever since. Jenny now lives deep in the heart of the farmland of Wales.